FOR THE LOVE OF TIA

DRAGON LORDS OF VALIDER NOVELLA (BOOK 4.1)

S. E. SMITH

ACKNOWLEDGMENTS

I would like to thank my husband Steve for believing in me and being proud enough of me to give me the courage to follow my dream. I would also like to give a special thank you to my sister and best friend, Linda, who not only encouraged me to write, but who also read the manuscript. Also to my other friends who believe in me: Julie, Jackie, Christel, Sally, Jolanda, Lisa, Laurelle, Debbie, and Narelle. The girls that keep me going!

And a special thanks to Paul Heitsch, David Brenin, Samantha Cook, Suzanne Elise Freeman, and PJ Ochlan—the awesome voices behind my audiobooks!

—S.E. Smith

ISBN: 9781691848836 (kdp paperback)
ISBN: 9781078745093 (BN paperback)
ISBN: 978-1-942562-34-4 (eBook)

Romance (love, suggestive sexual content) | Fantasy | Science Fiction (Aliens) | Royal | Contemporary | Paranormal | Novella | Action/Adventure

Published by Montana Publishing, LLC
& SE Smith of Florida Inc. www.sesmithfl.com

CONTENTS

SYNOPSIS

Tia is the Keeper of the Stories for the inhabitants of Glitter. She dreams of a life she knows will never happen, but hope blossoms when a strange creature is captured at the entrance to their kingdom, and Tia remembers the legend of the goddess that will renew their world.

Jett's thirst for adventure leads him to a previously undiscovered cavern where an unusual kingdom exists, and he is captivated by their beautiful Keeper. Unable to resist, he returns again and again until he knows he must steal her away.

CHAPTER ONE

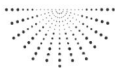

*T*ia sighed as she ran her delicate fingers over the smooth surface of the scroll. Her eyes stared blankly at the intricate illustrations and the symbols carefully describing each legend. Her tiny, light green ears flickered back and forth at the sound of rapidly approaching footsteps drawing her out of her trance. She knew immediately who it was – her brother Tamblin.

She quickly rolled the scroll and hid it behind one of the colorful fabric tapestries she had hanging in her room. She didn't want him to know that she had been writing down the stories of their people, at least not yet. He would be deeply concerned if he knew and become even more protective of her.

Tia closed her large brown eyes and drew in a deep breath in an effort to calm the fast beat of her heart. Every third beat, it would stop and she was terrified it would not start again. It was happening more often and lasting longer each time. She opened her eyes and forced a smile onto her face as her brother swept aside the long curtain door of her chambers.

"Tia, I have need of you," Tamblin said in his deep, rich voice.

"A creature has been captured at the entrance to our caverns. It is very large and strange-looking."

Tia tilted her head and frowned. "Why do you need me? Surely you do not expect me to give you my permission to kill it?" she asked scornfully. "You have never bothered to ask me before!" she pointed out, reminding him of the few times when an unknown creature wandered into their domain only to be killed within moments by the Guardians of the Cavern, two large WereBeast with poisonous saliva and barb-like fur.

Tamblin glared at her before straightening his broad shoulders. Even though he stood no taller than twelve inches tall, he was still taller than most of the other inhabitants of Glitter. As their ruler, he guarded the kingdom and its populaces with a fierce protectiveness that Tia knew she should appreciate more. A soft sigh escaped her. With her, he tended to be three times more protective, rarely letting her travel anywhere alone.

"Tia," he said, drawing in a deep breath to calm his frustration. "This creature is different from anything I have ever encountered before. The Guardians alerted us and we were able to render it unconscious before they attacked and killed it. As Keeper of the Stories, I thought it would be wise to seek your counsel first before I ordered it destroyed." He paused a moment and his eyes softened as he studied her. "I do respect your guidance, sister."

Tia lowered her eyes and blinked several times, ashamed of her unreasonable criticism. "I will come. Where is the creature now?"

"I have had it transported to the center of the moss field, near the river," Tamblin said, gently wrapping his hand around her arm. He frowned down at her in concern. "You have lost more weight. Have you not been feeling well again?"

Tia bit her lower lip with her sharp teeth and shook her head. "I'm fine, Tamblin. You have more important things to worry about than me," she assured him.

"Never, Tia," Tamblin responded quietly, guiding her out to the flying creatures they used as transport throughout the caverns. "You will always be the most important thing to me."

He helped her climb up onto the saddle that was strapped on the back of one of the bat-like creatures that lived in the caverns. Tia leaned forward and petted the body of the flying mammal that was covered in a thick, dark gray fur with large, black leathery wings. The winged animal turned and emitted a low humming noise when it saw Tia, its sharp pointed ears flicking back and forth in affection. Tamblin adjusted the tiny bridle and checked Tia's saddle to make sure she was comfortable.

"Tamblin," Tia said, leaning forward to touch her brother's shoulder before he moved away. She waited until he looked at her before she smiled. "Thank you."

"I love you, Tia," Tamblin said quietly. "I only want to keep you safe."

"I know," she responded lightly. "I know. Now, let us see what marvelous creature you have discovered."

Tia snapped the reins on her flying beast and drew in a shaky breath as it rose swiftly into the air. She loved flying. She loved the freedom. Sometimes when she had trouble breathing, she would close her eyes and imagine she was as free as the flying beasts were. It helped to calm the panic that rose inside her.

∾

"Jett," a soft whispered voice called out frantically. "You are going to get not only yourself killed but me too!"

Jett turned and grinned at the dark sand-colored face rushing up behind him. "Santil, if you are afraid of death, go back. I want to see the underground world again," he said with a silent laugh before turning to scoot through the narrow opening between the dark rocks.

"You want to see the female again, you mean," Santil growled out. "Did you not see the huge creatures that just flew into the cave? They could step on us and not even know it. We will be nothing but a pile of goo on the bottom of their feet."

Jett just shook his head. Santil was always looking at the gloomy side of things. Jett was the youngest son of the King of the Sand Kingdom. His thirst for adventure had gotten him into trouble more than once, but he loved the freedom of soaring over the sands, even if it meant being in danger of being eaten every once in a while.

Several months back, he and Santil had been flying over the sand dunes scouting for enemy worms that had attacked one of their military posts on the outer rim of their Kingdom. A small pod of the damn things had surprised them. Santil had been thrown off of his sand skimmer. Jett had engaged the worms and led them away. Unfortunately, he had encountered a large pod of them and was forced to seek shelter. That was how he found the small crack in the rocks that had led down to the most incredible kingdom under the sands.

And that is where I found my bride, he thought with satisfaction. *Now all I have to do is steal her away.*

Jett jumped down off the high rock face, landing on the smooth surface. He knew the tunnel by heart now. He had returned to it over and over since he discovered it, watching, waiting, wanting.

The first time he saw the delicate, green female he had been entranced by her beauty. Her large, dark brown eyes spoke of secrets he wanted to know. She moved like the sands dancing in the wind, barely touching the surface.

She always wore a gown that was made of the colors of the sky before a storm. His fingers itched to peel it from her slender figure. He wanted to run his lips around her tiny pointed ears and see if his whispered words of love would be returned.

He had no doubt in his mind that he loved her. She was with him every single moment whether he was awake or asleep. His mind could picture every small smile she gave to one of the many people of her clan that came to see her.

He loved to watch her as she studied the plants and mushroom shaped trees of her underground world. But he also worried that she would not care for the bright world of his kingdom. He feared she would not enjoy the sands or the fierce winds and storms that sometimes swept over his home.

"Well, are we going or are you going to stand there daydreaming all day?" Santil asked in irritation, jumping down to stand next to him.

Jett started when he realized that he had been dreaming instead of walking. He turned to look at Santil for a moment before turning his head to look down the dark tunnel. Making up his mind, he turned back to his friend once more.

"I want you to stay here," Jett commanded. "I will return in a few hours and when I do, I won't be alone. I plan to bring my bride with me."

Santil rolled his eyes in exasperation. "Don't you think you should ask her if she is interested in you first before you steal her away?"

Jett grinned at his friend. "What fun is there in that? Besides, what if she were to say no?"

Santil watched as his childhood friend sprinted down the dark tunnel, shaking his head in resignation. "How could she say no? No one ever has to you. Besides even if she did, you wouldn't listen." He chuckled as he talked to himself before jumping back up onto the ledge and leaning back against the rocky side so he could stare out at the bright sky waiting patiently for his friend to return.

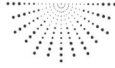

CHAPTER TWO

*T*ia stared in disbelief at the unconscious figure lying on the dark red moss. The stories flowed through her mind in vivid detail. She would never forget them. They were a part of her.

The legends spoke of a beautiful goddess with hair the color of white gold that would return life to their world. Several generations ago, giants from a distant world came in great ships and took the small creatures that fed on the minerals in the sand. The creatures, in return, had left their excreta that fertilized the planet, causing the growth of the huge mushroom forests.

When the last of the creatures were taken, their world began to die as there was nothing to fertilize the seeds buried deep within the sands. The vast forests of mushroom trees withered and died. The great storms that frequently developed grew worse because there were no forests to buffer their winds.

Soon, the sand began swallowing everything. What was worse was the giants had brought with them great worms that attacked Tia's people, killing most of her clan. Their only hope of salvation was to seek the protective walls of the rock caverns.

Over the last ten generations, they had developed their world until it was the beautiful kingdom that lay before her. Her body trembled as her heart jerked uncomfortably in her chest. Her last wish had been to see her people free to go to the surface, but she never believed that it would happen in her lifetime. Now, she knew that the gods had heard her desperate plea and were giving her this last gift before she died.

"What do you think, Tia," Tamblin asked quietly as he studied the still figure lying on the moss. "Should I order it destroyed?"

"NO!" Tia cried out, looking at him in horror before remembering he did not have the knowledge that she did, at least not yet. "No," she said in a quieter voice. "She has been sent by the gods and goddesses. She is the one. She has the knowledge to heal our world above so that we may live once more in the brightness."

Tamblin looked at Tia in disbelief before turning his head to look down at the figure that was now beginning to stir. He raised his hand in a silent command for his soldiers to be ready for anything. He would order the sharp spears, laced with the poison of the Guardians of the Cavern, to strike if the creature tried to attack.

How could the Gods or Goddesses send such a large creature as their salvation? He had listened to the stories his mother had told Tia when she didn't think he was listening. He could not see the stories in his head like his sister could, but he knew they were important.

Tamblin pushed Tia behind him when the creature slowly sat up. It was obvious the creature was female. She had many of the same features as their females did.

He watched suspiciously as she blinked several times before she glanced around her. His soldiers had taken to the air and were making careful sweeps around her, keeping just far enough away to stay out of her reach but close enough that they could launch the spears if need be. He straightened to his full height, refusing to cower in fear.

"Hello," the golden goddess said with a soft smile as her gaze settled on him and his sister.

Tia stepped nimbly around Tamblin to get a closer look at the giant female, but stopped at the husky sound of her voice. Tamblin moved swiftly next to Tia, scolding her to stay behind him. Tia ignored her brother. She knew deep down that the golden creature wouldn't hurt her.

"She will not harm me," she hissed out to her brother. "She is the one! I know it." She could see the images in her head of the golden goddess her mother told her would come to save their world.

Tamblin fought the urge to bundle his sister back up onto the flying beast and lock her away in the palace where he knew she was safe. He knew she was sick even as she tried to hide it from him. He could see the tremor in her hands, the weight she had lost, and how she had trouble breathing at times. He feared if she got too excited it might bring on an attack. He glanced worriedly from Tia's face to the creature who was sitting quietly waiting for them to respond to her.

Tamblin reluctantly nodded his head. He knew deep down that this was something he could not deny his sister. The golden goddess kept her hands on her thighs and waited as

Tia slowly approached her. Tia tilted her head again, her ears twitching to and fro when the creature spoke again. She might not understand her words but she did recognize the gentle tone.

≈

Tia stepped cautiously closer, reaching out and touching the larger female with the tips of her long green fingers. She smiled when the creature remained still. Feeling more confident, she moved a little closer.

Her heart pounded erratically when the female slowly raised one of her arms. She froze in fear, wondering if she could have been mistaken. As much as she was confident that this was the creature the stories told of, she was still unprepared for the size of it. Tia watched as the female slowly lowered one of her hands down onto the soft moss, palm upward. Tia looked back and forth between the palm and the creature's eyes before making the decision to trust her instincts.

She took a tentative step forward, stopping when Tamblin hissed out again in alarm. Shaking her head at him, she climbed up into the open palm. She couldn't resist running her slender fingers over the warm flesh of the creature.

It was soft and smooth – almost comforting. Tia glanced up and watched as the beautiful golden haired goddess nodded to her before carefully raising her hand, lifting Tia up into the air. Tia stood up, holding onto one of the long, slender fingers for balance and looked around her. Slowly, her people began to kneel down in reverence of the creature and Tia's courage to communicate with it. Only when her brother knelt as well did Tia turn to face the goddess who came from above with a smile on her tiny face.

≈

Jett slipped out of the dark passage and climbed down until he could see what was going on more clearly. The passage opened out near the smallest waterfall and onto the ledge that ran along the edge of it. It would be a quick climb down to the balcony of the palace where he often saw the slender green female standing and looking out over her kingdom.

His eyes suddenly widened in concern when he saw the huge golden giant sitting in the middle of the red moss field. A low growl escaped him and his hand tightened on the short sword he carried at his waist when he saw the creature lifting his bride. His lips drew back to show his small sharp teeth as he fought the urge to attack it. He would if it harmed the female he knew belonged to him. He didn't care how big it was, he would destroy it.

Moving along the side of the cliff, he nimbly began the climb down until he was a few feet above the balcony of the palace. He pushed off, landing silently on the spacious ledge. He turned as he landed, his knees bent and one hand stretched out to balance him before he stood. Moving into the shadows, he watched as the events below unfolded. He had to hide behind the thick curtains when three of the armed soldiers returned briefly to the palace only to return to his bride and the creature holding her in the palm of its huge hand.

Jett watched as his bride presented the creature with a glowing, red stone. He sucked in a breath when he realized he could understand what the creature was saying after she placed it around her neck.

"My name is Ariel," the creature replied with a soft chuckle.

"I am called Tia." Jett's breath left him in a hiss of painful desire when he heard Tia's name for the first time. He leaned forward, trying to get a better view. "I am the Keeper of the Stories. This is my brother, Tamblin. He is our leader," Tia replied in a silky voice that sent waves of heat rushing through him.

Jett smiled, Tia – a beautiful name for a beautiful woman. He continued to watch from his viewpoint, gaining confidence that the creature meant no harm to his bride or her people as he listened to her talk. He debated whether to follow when the creature stood and Tia, Tamblin, and many of his soldiers moved away but decided against it. They would return, of that he was confident.

No, now would be a good time to explore my bride's home and pack a few things that she might need, he decided.

Jett moved silently through the empty palace, exploring one level after another until he came to a room he knew must belong to Tia. He let the long curtain doorway fall behind him as he gently touched the delicate fabrics hanging on the walls. He breathed in, inhaling her fragrant scent. It made him think of the wild flowers that bloomed briefly after the heavy rains. He ran his tawny fingers over the silky woven lengths of cloth that she wrapped around her body. He couldn't help but imagine what it was going to be like when he unwove it from her slender frame.

Scooping up several long lengths, he quickly bundled them up so that they would be easy to carry. Inside of the bundle, he rolled the comb she used on her bright red hair and several delicate hair combs. He would have to make her more.

Combs made from the sands were beautiful and would look good against her silky strands. He pulled back the last tapestry hanging on the wall and discovered shelves filled with carefully rolled scrolls. Pulling out the one on top, he walked over to the low table in the center of the room and unrolled it. Inscribed on the thick fiber paper were images depicting different scenes. Each was done with delicate strokes filled with the same vibrant colors that reminded Jett of his beloved.

His eyes moved to the writing below them. He frowned as he concentrated. It was difficult, but he was slowly able to decipher the words. They were in the ancient language his mother and father taught him when he was young.

~

"What are you doing?" Tia's outraged voice sounded from the doorway. "Who are you? How did you get into my rooms?"

Jett had been so absorbed in deciphering the scroll and the tale it was telling that he had let his guard down. Now, instead of him having the element of surprise, his bride did. He took a quick step back from the table. He couldn't help but grin as his bride, upset that he had been reading her scroll, made the mistake of marching over to the table instead of calling for help or running away.

The moment she was within reach, he wrapped his arms around her trembling body. "Do not fear, my heart. I have not come to harm you, but to claim you," he breathed out in her ear.

Tia jerked in surprise, her eyes widening as she stared up at him, startled. "What do you mean - claim me?" she asked, bewildered.

Jett chuckled at her innocent look of confusion. He couldn't resist leaning down and brushing his lips briefly against hers. Her startled gasp pulled a groan from him and he took her lips in a savage kiss that spoke of his desire. He had wanted to do this since he first saw her several months ago.

Tia pushed weakly against his broad chest until he reluctantly lifted his head. "What do you think you are doing?" she gasped breathlessly, looking up at him with huge, confused eyes.

Jett smiled mischievously. "I thought that was a bit obvious! I'm claiming you as my bride."

CHAPTER THREE

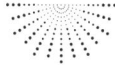

*T*ia didn't know how to respond to the larger male who had invaded her personal domain. She had never seen anyone like him before. He was tall, even taller than her brother. He was also not the same soft shade of green that most of her clan was.

He was a dark, tawny color with rich dark brown hair that fell in long, braided ropes down his back almost to his waist. His eyes were a light violet, almost identical to the water that flowed from the rocky walls of their home. He did not wear clothing like them, either. A blush heightened the color of her cheeks as her hands slid over the bare flesh of his shoulders. The only thing covering him was a pair of light brown pants tucked into a darker brown pair of ankle boots.

"I am not your bride," Tia snapped out, upset that she let this strange man shake her normal calm. "You will leave immediately or I will summon my brother and the guards!"

Jett grinned down at her, letting his hands span her tiny waist. "Of course, my lady, I will be happy to leave immediately," he said with a playful kiss to her lips.

He chuckled at Tia's outraged gasp when he lifted her gently up and balanced her on his shoulder so he could grab the things he had packed for her in his other hand. Keeping his arm around her thighs, he listened carefully before drawing the curtain leading out to the balcony aside. He jumped up onto the ledge, balancing before he murmured for her to hang on and not fight him.

"What are you doing?" Tia gasped again as she stared fearfully down at the long drop to the ground below them. She tried to cling to him, but didn't have any way to really hold on so she remained frozen. "You are going to kill us!" she whispered hoarsely.

Jett laughed as he nimbly began climbing up the side of the cliff to the ledge where the crack to the tunnel was. "You haven't been talking with Santil, have you? He said the same thing!"

Tia frowned, thinking hard before she shook her head. "I don't know a Santil. Where does he live?" she asked, unable to contain her curiosity.

"In the Kingdom of the Sand People," Jett replied, pulling himself up far enough to set her down on the ledge before he pulled himself up onto it. "That is where I am taking you."

Tia looked at the huge tawny figure standing over her with her mouth opened. He really meant it when he said he was claiming her. Her heart did a little quiver and began to beat faster, but for once she wondered if it was because of her sickness or because of his words.

She looked out over the cavern filled with the richness of the mushroom forests and the glittering stones that gave them life. The thought of leaving her safe world should have terrified her but it didn't. Her eyes moved to look up at the powerful figure standing over hers and inside she felt a wave of longing.

She knew she didn't have long to live. She had resigned herself to live her remaining time quietly reviewing the stories she had illustrated and retold. The fact that she would not live long enough to have children of her own caused a sharp pain to flair through her.

Her death would mean the end of the line of the Keeper of the Stories. That was why she felt it was so important to pass on her knowledge the only way she could. Her eyes traveled down to the balcony to her rooms.

She had finished all the stories that she knew. There really was nothing left for her here. Perhaps, this was the gods and goddesses way of letting her see what was beyond her home before her heart no longer beat.

Jett stepped closer to where she was sitting and knelt on one knee before her. He brushed a strand of her wayward hair back tenderly before cupping her chin. He waited until her eyes once more looked deeply into his.

"Come with me," he whispered, holding out his hand. "Let me show you my world."

Tia bit her lip and studied him for a moment before she let her eyes sweep over the cavern one last time. "I didn't get to say goodbye to Tamblin," she answered reluctantly.

"It is not goodbye," Jett promised her. "I will bring you back whenever you wish to visit."

Tia knew deep down there would be no coming back once she left. She knew Tamblin would be upset when he discovered her missing. She could only hope that he would understand when he saw the scrolls and read through them. When he did, he would discover the note she had left for him among them.

She had not planned on him finding it before her death, but what did it matter whether she was dead or not. In the end, it would not change her outcome.

Tia turned back to look at the unusual, but handsome male kneeling in front of her and laid her trembling hand in his strong, firm one. "I will come with you," she breathed out with a small excited smile.

Jett leaned in, brushing his lips across hers before pulling her up with a joyful laugh. "You will not regret it, I swear. I will show you the most wondrous sights!" he exclaimed joyfully as he wrapped his hands around her tiny waist and lifted her up, swinging her around with a shout of joy.

Tia laughed breathlessly as he set her back onto her feet. He gripped her hand firmly but gently in his and pulled her toward the narrow opening. Tia glanced back briefly over her shoulder as he pulled her through before focusing on the new path she was taking.

CHAPTER FOUR

*S*antil shook his head when he saw Jett emerge out of the darkness with a slender green female. "You are going to start a war, you know," Santil said with a sigh.

Jett laughed, looking down in amusement at Tia. "Meet Santil. He is always thinking the worse is going to happen."

"That is because it usually does," Santil snorted, scowling. "Jett is forever getting us in trouble."

"Jett," Tia said softly with a smile. "I like that name," she said shyly, staring up at the huge male that took her breath away.

Santil stopped at the opening of the tunnel and looked at his large friend in disbelief. "You kidnapped her and didn't even bother to tell her your name? That is low, even for you, my friend," he joked before turning back to make sure the coast was clear of any predators.

"Ignore him," Jett teased back, jumping down behind his friend and opening his arms for her. "I try to." Tia couldn't help but giggle at the way the two unusual men picked on each other.

It was so different from Tamblin and the elders. Only the children seemed to have a sense of humor anymore, she thought sadly.

Tia shielded her eyes from the brightness that she had only heard about. She had never seen the top side of their world. Tamblin had refused her many requests, saying it was too dangerous. She blinked rapidly until her eyes adjusted enough so that she could see without her eyes tearing.

It was big and beautiful. As far as she could see there were rolling waves of glittering, windswept sand. She tried to imagine what it would have looked like before when the large mushroom forests covered it but couldn't.

"Come," Jett said with a soft smile of encouragement. "We need to make haste if we are to return to our home before the darkness falls."

Santil shuddered. "I agree. I don't want to have to deal with the night creatures on top of everything else."

"What else is there?" Tia asked curiously as she put her hands on Jett's broad shoulder to steady herself as he lowered her down to the ground.

A warm shiver swept down her spine and she couldn't resist looking up at him to see if he felt her reaction. The heated look in his eyes showed he was not immune to her touch either. A rosy blush rose up her cheeks as unfamiliar feelings coursed through her.

"Sand worms," Jett and Santil said at the same time, answering the question she had already forgotten she had asked.

"But, you needn't worry," Jett said, guiding her to a small machine with a long seat and odd shaped wings. He helped her on before sliding behind her so he could keep one arm wrapped protectively around her. "I'll keep you safe," he murmured in her ear enjoying how the tiny points twitched and a light dusky rose color flushed her cheeks.

~

Tia loved the journey to the Kingdom of the Sand. It had taken them until dusk to reach it. Her first view had been of the huge clear, glittering dome set upon a high rocky surface. As they skimmed across the sands, more details began to emerge. She could see the shape of a huge castle built into the center of the rock face. It was surrounded by large turrets on each corner.

Tia pressed a hand to her chest as her heart stuttered and stopped. She tried to draw in a deep breath, but couldn't. The hand gripping Jett's arm tightened in panic as she feared her time had come to an end just when she was getting a chance to experience her first true adventure. Jett's arm squeezed her and she felt his warm breath against her neck just as her heart restarted sluggishly at first before picking up its uneven rhythm again.

"Welcome to Sandora," Jett whispered in her ear.

Tia nodded, unable to speak for the lump in her throat. Instead, she squeezed his arm to let him know she heard him. The light skimmers sped down a long tunnel that opened up at their approach. Tia looked over her shoulder trying to see but couldn't because of Jett's larger frame.

"The tunnel collapses behind us so nothing else can come in behind us," he explained with an understanding smile. "Hang on," he said.

He tightened his hold on her before pushing down his feet on the accelerator, sending the skimmer speeding through the tunnel until it burst through high above the walls of the city below them. He shouted with joy as he flew in and out of the narrow tubes that formed walkways between buildings. He didn't slow down until he reached the outer corridor leading into the palace.

They swept through a long, dark tunnel before coming out into a wide area filled with men, women, and skimmers. Santil floated down beside them a moment later with a huge grin on his face. Jett jumped off the skimmer, sweeping Tia up into his arms.

Tia squealed in alarm before wrapping her arms tightly around his neck. "I can walk," she said breathlessly even as she snuggled closer to his warm body.

Jett smiled tenderly down at her and shook his head, sending his long braids dancing around him in waves. "I know but I like carrying you," he teased. "I don't ever want to put you down."

Tia rolled her big brown eyes at him. "You would just tire yourself out," she snorted but couldn't quite hide her amused smile.

"I'd like to see that!" Santil said, coming up beside them and slapping Jett on the back of his head before dancing away out of Jett's reach. "His mother, father, sister, and brothers have been trying to do that since the day he was born!"

"Like you are any better!" Jett retorted with a playful snap of his teeth.

"Jett!" a loud, deep voice called out harshly.

Santil grimaced before raising his hand and saluting Jett and Tia. "That is my signal to disappear. It has been a pleasure to meet the one who could capture this mongrel's attention, my lady," he said before disappearing between two outer buildings.

Tia watched wide-eyed as a figure as imposing as Jett's

walked down a set of steps towards them. The man was dressed in a pair of dark brown pants with a black vest that left much of his chest exposed. Around his waist he carried two swords that swayed as he strode toward them. His hair was as long as Jett's and braided in long dark brown ropes that flowed gracefully behind him as he walked.

"Who is that?" she asked in a hushed whisper, watching the huge male approach with a fierce scowl upon his face.

"My father," Jett grinned. "He only looks scary, but he really isn't."

Tia ducked her head to hide her giggle before she raised it to look at the man as he came to a stop in front of them. "Who is this?" Roan asked, looking at Tia with a puzzled expression on his face. "Why is she green?"

Tia looked at the man with a stubborn tilt to her chin. "Why aren't you?" she asked back with a raised eyebrow.

Roan stared at the female for a moment before he burst out laughing. "I have no idea. I will have to ask my mother," he responded in amusement. "Roan, King of the Sand Kingdom at your service," he added with a graceful bow.

Tia giggled. "I am called Tia. Keeper of the Stories for the Kingdom of Glitter," she responded with a shy smile. "It is indeed a pleasure to meet you, your Grace."

"Jett?" Roan asked, staring into Tia's unusual but beautiful face.

"I've claimed her," Jett responded to the unspoken question. "She is my bride."

Roan started in surprise before a large grin lit his face up. "At last," he murmured before he turned and bellowed out in a voice that ricocheted around the high walls of the palace. "Jett has taken a bride!" he proclaimed to all standing within hearing distance.

Loud cheers followed his announcement, stunning Tia who stared in awe as men and women gathered around them cheering. "What is going on?" she whispered, trying to sink down into Jett's arms. "What did he mean, you have taken a bride? I heard you say that before, but I am not familiar with the word," she said, looking nervously up at him.

Jett leaned over and whispered in her ear so she could hear him above the roar of the crowds. Tia paled as the meaning sank in. She looked up at him, tears filling her eyes as the realization of what was happening overwhelmed her.

She had to tell him it was impossible. There was no way she could be his bride as much as she wished she could be. She did not understand how it worked for his people, but for hers the loss of a mate could have devastating consequences.

Her heart beat frantically, stuttering and stopping before repeating the erratic rhythm over and over until she was trembling and had turned a deathly pale green. Her eyes drooped at the effort to keep them open. Her breath came in tiny gasps as her weak heart worked frantically in her chest.

"My lords! Strangers approach!" one of the guards yelled down.

Tia felt her vision blurring and tried to calm the panic. Her heart slowed, but continued to skip, leaving her weak. She turned to stare up at the top of the clear dome, recognizing the flying beast from home and the colors of her brother's armor. Turning her head, she let it fall weakly back against Jett's broad chest, seeking comfort from his strength.

Roan turned to look up at the clear dome as well. Even in the dim light, he could see the flying creatures with warriors guiding them as they hovered around the top of the Kingdom. He ordered his men to their skimmers and to prepare for battle.

"Wait!" Jett's voice rose over the mayhem. "What did you say, Tia?" he asked, concerned by her sudden pale complexion.

"It is Tamblin," she said weakly. "I must… see him… one… last… time," she murmured in a voice barely loud enough to be heard.

"Tia, what is it, my love? What do you mean one last time? What is wrong?" Jett asked fearfully, pulling her closer to his chest as he gazed down at her pale complexion.

Tia forced her eyes open so she could look into Jett's handsome features. "I'm dying," she forced out. "I…" Tears filled her eyes and overflowed down her pale cheeks. "I…. cannot be…. your bride."

$\approx$

"No," Jett cried out hoarsely, looking to his father who heard the quiet words. "No, she cannot die. I love her," he croaked out to his father in fear.

Roan looked at his son's ashen face before gazing at the slender figure cradled protectively against his youngest son's body. "There is a way to save her. Take her to the healing chamber," he said, his face set in determination. He turned to his head guard. "Open the tunnel," he ordered as he climbed onto his skimmer.

Jett watched his father rise up to fly over the walls of the palace. He pulled Tia closer to his body and strode for the entrance. He looked up at the door as he climbed the steps. His mother stood looking down at him with tears of compassion glimmering in her eyes. He felt her hand brush over his arm gently as he passed her.

"She will live if that is your decision," his mother said quietly.

"It is," Jett said, striding down the long corridor toward the entrance to the healing chambers buried deep under the palace.

≈

Tia drifted in and out of consciousness as her tiny heart struggled. Jett's tender touch soothed her fears and a sense of peace settled over her. She would not be alone when she died. That had been one of her greatest fears. She heard voices in the background. At times they rose in anger before a gentle voice spoke.

"You understand what this means," Roan said heavily as he looked at his son.

"Jett?" His mother reached out and touched his arm in fear and worry.

Jett turned his head to look at his mother and shook his head. "You do not understand. I knew the moment I saw her, she was for me."

Tamblin stepped forward; helpless rage twisted his features as he stared at the pale face of his beloved sister. "What do you mean she was for you? You did not even know her until today!" he bit out angrily. "Why did you take her? The excitement of being taken from her home is too much for her. Return her to me and let me take her home. At least she will die among her people!"

"No," Jett said, rising angrily and pulling his sword. "She is mine and will remain by my side!"

"What can you do?" Tamblin yelled as he took a step closer to Jett. "What can you do that we haven't? There is nothing we can do to save her," he said, anger and grief choking him as he stared at the tall male who stood protectively over Tia.

Jett's jaw clenched and he looked at the glowing waters of their healing pool. As with all things in life, there had to be a balance with death. There could not be one without the other. The healing pools demanded such balance. The healing waters would not work if the balance was not maintained. Jett could not ask another to give their life in exchange for Tia. The only way the pools could save one as sick as her was if another life was sacrificed so that its power was replenished, keeping the balance between life and death.

Jett looked at Tamblin before turning to gaze tenderly down at Tia's still form. "I would give anything to save her," he responded quietly before letting his sword drop to the floor of the chamber. "I would give anything… including my life."

Tamblin fell backwards in confusion at the sudden change in the male in front of him. Jett didn't give Tia's brother a chance to protest. He gently scooped Tia up into his arms, smiling down at her still, pale face. He bent his head closer to her and brushed a soft kiss over her lips.

"I love you, Tia," he murmured quietly, forgetting everyone else in the large chamber. "I give to you my heart, so that it may beat strongly for you. I give to you my strength so you never feel weak, and I give to you my love, so you will know the joy you have given me by just existing."

Jett walked down the steps and into the swirling blue and silver waters of the pool, moving slowly until it covered Tia up to her chin. Taking a deep breath, he pressed his lips against hers one last time and slowly sank down under the shimmering surface.

CHAPTER FIVE

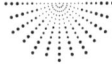

*T*ia felt waves of warmth flowing through her body. At first, she thought it was strange as she had been so cold before. Her heartbeat grew stronger as the warmth encircled her. She could feel Jett surrounding her with his love as well as his arms.

Shimmering lights danced behind her eyelids as images of them together formed. It was as if she could see their life together. His eyes turning with laughter to her as he held one of their children in his strong arms as another clung to his leg.

She could feel his strong arms holding her in the darkness as he listened to her tell him of her visions. She could feel the joy of him taking her on his skimmer through the lush mushroom forests that would soon cover their world again. In those few precious moments, she saw what she thought she would never have.

Tia felt strength suffusing her. It filled her body and a sense of peace and happiness at being whole again swept through her. She fought the urge to cry out when the lips pressed against hers suddenly fell away, waking her from the web of dreams she had been caught in. She opened her eyes under the swirling water, her feelings of joy turning to fear and despair when she saw Jett's still, peaceful face floating before her.

Her hands went frantically to his face, cupping his cheeks and holding him. Fear unlike anything she had ever known made her press her lips to his in a desperate attempt to wake him even as her hands moved to his chest. Under her palms, his heart stuttered and stilled.

NO! she screamed silently. *I won't let you do this. I love you. You claimed me,* she sobbed silently. *How can I be your bride if you are not with me? How can my dreams become reality without you by my side? How can you hold our children if you are not there to give them to me? Please, no. Please, please, please, don't leave me alone,* she begged, pressing her lips frantically to his again in an effort to give him back what he had given to her. *I don't want your gift without you. You promised me strength, but I am weak without your arms around me. You promised me joy, but there is nothing but sadness without you there to make me laugh. You promised me your heart, but without you it is empty. Please come back to me. I love you. Only together can I be strong. Only together can I find joy. Only together can we find love.*

Tia closed her eyes, wrapping her arms and legs around Jett's still, lifeless body. She gave herself to the swirling waters. She had no desire to live a half-life. If the gods and goddesses would take his life in exchange for hers then she would give them both of their souls so they could be as one for eternity.

Twisting her fingers through his long, braided ropes of hair, she let their bodies sink further under the dark blue and silver liquid. A sense of peace and acceptance settled over her. She would not die alone and she would not leave him.

"Keeper of the Stories," a soothing voice echoed through her mind and resonated through her soul. *"Do you not remember the story of the great warrior?"*

Tia stirred as the vivid images flooded her mind. Imagines of a great warrior who was said to have fallen in love with a gentle girl from another tribe. Her mother's voice flowed over her as the pictures danced through her mind.

"Remember, Tia," her mother scolded her when she drifted off instead of paying attention. "Only when the warrior gives the ultimate sacrifice will the gods and goddesses gift them with their hearts' desire."

"What is that, momma?" a tiny Tia asked, turning her large brown eyes in curiosity to her mother.

"He will give his heart to save her and she will refuse to accept it unless he keeps it safe for her," her mother replied, stroking her hair.

"Does that make her a warrior too?" the childlike Tia asked. "If she fights for him, will that make her a warrior?"

"Of course, little one," her mother said soothingly. "How can there be love if only one heart beats?"

Tia felt her body drifting upward, carried by the strong arms that surrounded her. *I remember, momma,* she thought. *I remember.*

Tia's eyes fluttered open as the healing waters fell away from her. She stared up into the light violet eyes of Jett, who smiled tenderly down at her as he carried her out of the healing pool. She reached a trembling hand up to lightly trace his cheek with her fingertips. An answering smile curved her lips.

"You are my warrior," she murmured in awe, her eyes shining with love. "You are the warrior who would give his heart to me."

Jett gazed down into her softly glowing eyes. "I would do anything for your love, Tia," he said huskily. "You are my life."

"As you are mine," Tia replied, knowing that the vision she had of their life together would soon become a reality.

Author's Note: I hope you enjoyed the story of Tia and Jett. These characters were first introduced in Ambushing Ariel: Dragon Lords of Valdier Book 4. I never expected to write them into Ariel's story, but once I did, I became fascinated with their characters. I feel all characters deserve to have their stories told if they wish to share it with me. Perhaps Tamblin might wish to share his story as well. I hope so.

~ S. E. Smith

See your favorite characters again in:
The Dragonlings and the Magic Four-Leaf Clover

A little magic can go a long way....

A campfire tale has the dragonlings and their besties enchanted with a mythical kingdom called Glitter, home of the magical, mischievous Great King Leprechaun and the Little People. When their dads disappear, they are certain King Leprechaun is responsible. Armed with a magic four-leaf clover, the younglings will do anything to save their fathers, including tricking the King by using their golden symbiots—because everyone knows a Leprechaun can't resist gold!

Check out the full novella here:
books2read.com/Dragonlings-Magic-Four-Leaf-Clover

Or for something new, S.E. Smith recommends:

First Awakenings
A Project Gliese 581G Novel

Ash has always embraced adventure and women, but when he wakes on an alien planet, there's no time for anything other than survival – or so he thinks.

Kella Ta'Qui is Turbinta – a member of the guild that discards their genetic identities in favor of what they train to become: assassins. Her first mission is to find and kill whoever was inside the foreign pod that landed on Tesla Terra, but predator becomes prey when she is wounded by her target. Dazed and confused, she stumbles into a group who plan to sell her to the highest bidder – until a rescuer appears. When Kella discovers that she owes her freedom to the target of her botched mission, things get interesting!

There is a bigger picture at stake, however. Forces beyond Kella and Ash are ramping up for a full-scale war, and as usual, when there's trouble, Ash is right in the middle of it.

Check out the full book here:
books2read.com/First-Awakenings

ADDITIONAL STORIES

If you loved this story by me (S.E. Smith) please leave a review!

You can discover additional books at http://sesmithya.com. There you can also sign up for my newsletter to hear about my latest releases!

Find your favorite way to keep in touch below:

Newsletter direct link: http://eepurl.com/bBgI6v

RSS Feed: http://feeds.feedburner.com/MyFeedName

Facebook: https://facebook.com/YABooksSESmith

Twitter: https://twitter.com/SESmithYA

Pinterest: https://www.pinterest.com/SESmithYA/

Youtube: https://goo.gl/AjsvBt

Tumblr: http://sesmithya.tumblr.com/

Instagram: https://instagram.com/sesmithya/

Epic Science Fiction / Action Adventure

Project Gliese 581G Series

An international team leave Earth to investigate a mysterious object in our solar system that was clearly made by someone, someone who isn't from Earth. Discover new worlds and conflicts in a sci-fi adventure sure to become your favorite!

First Awakenings

Survivor Skills

New Adult / Young Adult

Breaking Free Series

Makayla steals her grandfather's sailboat and embarks on a journey that will challenge everything she has ever believed about herself.

Voyage of the Defiance

Capture of the Defiance

Makayla is older now, but when she needs help, her friends from years ago join new and unexpected allies. Capture of the Defiance is a thriller mystery that stands on its own as danger reveals itself in sudden, heart-stopping moments.

The Dust Series

Fragments of a comet hit Earth, and Dust wakes to discover the world as he knew it is gone. It isn't the only thing that has changed, though, so has Dust…

Dust: Before and After (Book 1)

Dust: A New World Order (Book 2)

Dragonlings of Valdier

The Valdier, Sarafin, and Curizan Lords had children who just cannot stop getting into trouble! There is nothing as cute or funny as magical, shapeshifting kids, and nothing as heartwarming as family.

The Dragonlings and the Magic Four-Leaf Clover

ABOUT THE AUTHOR

S.E. Smith is an *internationally acclaimed*, *New York Times* **and** *USA TODAY Bestselling* author of science fiction, romance, fantasy, paranormal, and contemporary works for adults, young adults, and children. She enjoys writing a wide variety of genres that pull her readers into worlds that take them away.

Made in the USA
Monee, IL
21 September 2020